Something Wicked

by Anne Schraff

W0008317

Perfection Learning® Corporation
Logan, Iowa 51546

Cover Design: Mark Hagenberg

Cover Image Credit: Photodisc (Royalty-free)

For information, contact:
Perfection Learning® Corporation
1000 North Second Avenue, P.O. Box 500,
Logan, Iowa 51546-0500.
Phone: 1-800-831-4190 • Fax: 1-800-543-2745
perfectionlearning.com

Paperback ISBN 0-7891-6668-2
Reinforced Library Binding ISBN 0-7569-4765-0

2 3 4 5 6 PP 10 09 08 07 06

1 KIM HYUN TRAN RACED from drama class, bursting with excitement.

"Arnetta," she hollered as soon as she spotted her best friend. "I'm going to be Lady Macbeth!" she cried. "Can you believe it?"

A big grin broke on Arnetta's ebony face as the girls hugged and danced around in a circle. "You got the greatest role in the play *Macbeth*? Of course I believe it!" Arnetta said. "You're the best actress in the drama club, and Mr. Gabriel knows it. He's no fool!"

"Oh, Arnetta, I'm so thrilled. I would have been happy to play one of the witches, but Lady Macbeth is the best part! What a juicy role. It's going to be so much fun!"

"Who got Macduff?" Arnetta asked.

"Tyler Kern, that new boy from up north. He's nice," Kim said.

"You've got a funny look on your face. Something tells me Rodney Ormsley got Macbeth," Arnetta said.

Kim giggled nervously. "Yeah, I was hoping somebody else would get the role. Rodney is kind of . . . I don't know."

"He's arrogant, stuck on himself, and impossible," Arnetta finished the sentence. "He really wants to be an actor."

"It'll be okay, though," Kim said. "He's got a wonderful voice, and he is a good actor. I think we'll get along." Nothing could undermine Kim's happiness at being chosen to play Lady Macbeth. She was sure that Rodney would work very hard to get along with everybody just to make the play a success.

Kim walked to her locker in the early afternoon, still giddy about the play. She needed to grab her history book to study that evening. She was determined not to let her happiness over *Macbeth* cause her to ignore her other subjects.

As Kim approached her locker, she saw a note taped to the outside. Kim smiled. It was probably the work of her boyfriend, Huong Lam, who was a senior at Susan B. Anthony High School. Both Kim's family and Huong's came from the Mekong River Delta in Vietnam. Kim and Huong had both grown up in America, but their grandparents had been neighbors in Vietnam and shared many memories. Huong was always writing funny notes and taping them to Kim's locker. Kim figured by now he knew about her playing Lady Macbeth, and he had a joke about it already.

Still smiling, Kim pulled the note off and opened it up. But it was not Huong's handwriting. It wasn't in anybody's handwriting. It had been written on a computer.

> "Fair is foul, and foul is fair,
> I cast spells, my wrath beware.
> If you play the Lady Macbeth,
> You might soon run out of breath."

The smile faded from Kim's face. What kind of a sick joke was this? Kim didn't know anyone who would want to upset her like this by making a stupid threat. Only two other girls had even been considered for the role of Lady Macbeth—Pamela Morgan and Beth Skinner. But neither of them seemed very upset when they got other, lesser roles.

Kim looked around the crowded hallway

where other students were pulling books and binders from their lockers. Anthony High was a new school with an excellent reputation for scoring high in the state-wide achievement tests. The student body included African American, Hispanic, Asian, and Middle Eastern kids along with those of European backgrounds. Everybody seemed to get along well together. Kim racked her brain for someone who would have such a wicked sense of humor. She couldn't come up with anybody.

Kim's first impulse was to bunch up the note and toss it in the trash. She was a firm believer in not letting destructive people interfere with her life. But she was a little worried. If there was some bad person trying to undermine her, or the play, she thought her drama teacher, Mr. Gabriel, should know about it.

Kim walked back to the drama classroom where Mr. Gabriel was still at his desk. He was a darkly handsome man with intense, black eyes and thick, wavy hair. His mother was born in India and his father in England. When he wasn't teaching drama to high school students, he played small parts on television or in Shakespearean festivals. Kim felt very lucky to have such a teacher.

"Mr. Gabriel," Kim said, "I found this note on my locker just now. I know it's probably a silly joke of some kind, but it bothered me."

Mr. Gabriel stood up. "Oh? Let me see it," he said.

Kim handed him the note, and he read it. Then reread it. "The first part is the opening verse in Act I. I can't imagine who would have written it. You say it was on your locker?" he asked.

"Yes, just now. I thought maybe somebody who wanted to be Lady Macbeth and didn't get it was mad or something," Kim said, thinking out loud.

"Both girls I had considered didn't seem to want the role badly. I suspect the writer of that inane verse is some joker who is bored with life around here. I wouldn't worry about it, Kim. We've got our share of clowns in this school, unfortunately." He handed the note back to Kim.

Kim smiled. "That's what I thought too. Oh, Mr. Gabriel, I am so excited about the play. I think it will be great."

Mr. Gabriel was a very demanding teacher but so skilled that his students respected him. "It will be great if the actors are relentless in their preparation. I am counting on you to be a formidable Lady Macbeth, Kim," he said.

Kim left the classroom and bunched up the note before tossing it in the trash. Mr. Gabriel was right. Even though Anthony High had a large share of very good students, it had its share of silly people too.

"Kim," Huong said as he came around the corner, "I heard the news! Congratulations!"

Kim flew into Huong's arms, and he gave her a big hug. "I am going to do such a great job that you will be proud of me, Huong. I'll make my parents and my whole family proud. Oh, it makes me shiver when I think of being on stage and everybody watching me as Lady Macbeth!"

"I'm already proud of you," Huong said. His eyes danced when he laughed. Kim thought Huong Lam had the happiest face of any boy she ever knew. It was one of the things she loved about him.

As Kim and Huong walked toward the bus that would take them home, Rodney Ormsley approached in the opposite direction. "Hi, Kim," he said, his face very serious. "I'm going to talk to Mr. Gabriel about our costumes. Everything has to be just right. No rummaging around that old prop room in the basement for rags left over from other plays. We need everything to be perfect. There could very well be important people in the audience watching the play. This could be a springboard for some of our careers."

As much as Kim loved acting, she didn't want to pursue it as a career. She loved science too, and she hoped to go into medical research or perhaps be a doctor. "I know everything will be fine," she said, giggling a little. When she was with people who intimidated her, Kim sometimes giggled. Rodney was one of those people.

"This play is not a laughing matter, you know," Rodney said sternly. "I hope you realize how important it is that you do well as Lady Macbeth, Kim. It's a pivotal role. If you blow it, then you've ruined the whole play."

"Oh, I'll rehearse until I get it down perfectly," Kim promised.

When they reached the bus stop, Huong looked at Kim. "I don't know about this role, Kim. You have such a cute, sweet little face and such gentle eyes. How can you play this evil, conniving woman who pushes her husband to murder someone? Think you can really pull it off?" he said teasingly.

Kim had already memorized some of her lines, and now she made her expression as grim as she could. She hissed at Huong, "Screw your courage to the sticking place, and we shall not fail!" It was Lady Macbeth urging her husband on to murder.

Huong whistled. "I don't know if you can scare the audience, but you've sure scared me!" he said, laughing.

....

Kim's parents both worked as accountants in their own business, but her mother was always home after school. She liked to be home to greet Kim and her younger brother Sham.

"Guess what?" Kim shouted as she

walked in the house. "I got the part!"

"Wow," Sham said, "I thought you'd be one of the witches, Kim."

Kim gave her brother a friendly punch and said, "Mom, I'm so excited. It's such a wonderful character. Lady Macbeth is wicked, but she has such depth . . . "

"I'm glad for you, Kim," her mom said, "but it will be a lot of work. You'll have to spend many afternoons rehearsing. Have you planned for that?"

"I don't mind. I've already finished two big projects in English and science that aren't due for two weeks," Kim said. "Tyler Kern, that new boy I told you about—the quiet one—he's playing Macduff."

"Who's playing old Macbeth himself?" Sham asked.

"Rodney Ormsley," Kim said. "He's not my favorite person in the whole school, but he's very good. It'll be exciting pitting my dialogue against his. He's so good he'll bring out the best in me." Kim left out the part about Rodney already lecturing Kim to work hard.

Once Kim got to her room, she began work on a history paper that wasn't due for three weeks. She wanted to get that out of the way too so she could concentrate on Macbeth.

The phone rang just as Kim sat down at the computer. Kim's parents had given her a phone for her 16th birthday two months earlier.

"Hello," Kim said, thinking it was somebody else calling to congratulate her on getting the role of Lady Macbeth.

But whoever was on the other end of the line said nothing.

"Who is this?" Kim asked.

The voice, when it came, seemed disguised. Someone was speaking in a strange, hoarse voice.

"Fire burn and cauldron bubble, I cast spells of dire trouble. If you play Lady Macbeth, be prepared to welcome death." The phone went dead. Kim stared at it, shocked. Why would anyone do such a thing? If it was a joke, it wasn't the least bit funny.

Kim always talked everything over with her parents. But she couldn't tell them about this. It would frighten them. They had come to America as teenagers, but they still remembered the fear and terror they saw around them in their flight to freedom. They would take the warnings seriously. They would insist on Kim dropping out of the play. She couldn't do that.

It was a dream come true for Kim to play Lady Macbeth, and she wasn't about to give that up.

2 KIM CALLED ARNETTA and told her about the note on her locker and the telephone call. "Who do we know who'd be sick enough to do something like that?" Kim asked.

"You need to tell Mr. Gabriel about it," Arnetta said. She wasn't treating the matter as lightly as Kim thought she might. Kim would have felt better if Arnetta had laughed it off. Arnetta's seriousness made Kim more nervous.

"I already told him about the first note, and he said some clown must have written it just for excitement," Kim said.

"Was it a guy or a girl on the phone?" Arnetta asked.

"I couldn't even tell," Kim said. "The person was changing their voice so much that it could have been either. I kind of think it was a guy, or maybe a girl who could make her voice really deep . . . "

"My guess is that one of those other girls who was up for the role is upset, Kim," Arnetta said. "It's something some jealous girl might do. Deep down, one of the girls who lost the part really cared a lot, and this is her way of getting back at you."

"Pamela and Beth have always been nice to me, Arnetta. I can't imagine either of them doing something like this. I mean, when Mr. Gabriel announced that I'd be playing Lady Macbeth, they both came up and gave me big hugs," Kim said.

"Girls can really be two-faced, Kim," Arnetta said. "Pamela wants to be an actress very badly, and she's Rodney's girlfriend. Playing Lady Macbeth would have given her a lot more time to be with him. Now you get to do all that stuff with Rodney. Maybe that bothers her, and she doesn't want to be up front about it."

"You think she'd go so far as to try to scare me into dropping out of the play?" Kim asked.

"There used to be a radio show that my grandpa listened to. He's got cassettes of it. There was a spooky-voiced guy at the beginning who always said, 'who knows what evil lurks in the minds of men?' Well, I guess he meant women too," Arnetta said.

"Well," Kim said, "nobody is going to

scare me away from doing this play. I'm not some weak little wimp who runs away scared at the sight of trouble. I come from a family that braved wars and typhoons to come to America and make a new life. Some stupid little threat isn't going to get me to drop out of *Macbeth*."

....

When Kim arrived at school the next day, she headed straight for her history class. Pamela, Beth, and Rodney were in that class too. Pamela always sat by Rodney. They made no secret of the fact that they liked each other. Pamela was very pretty, and Rodney was handsome. They were both in love with drama. Kim thought that it would be only natural if Rodney wished Pamela had gotten the role of Lady Macbeth instead of Kim.

Kim felt ill at ease talking to Pamela, even though up until now they had had a good, friendly relationship. They weren't best friends or anything, but Kim had never felt awkward around her like she did now. Thinking that Pamela might be behind those nasty messages lurked in Kim's mind.

"Hi, Kim," Pamela said. "Have you looked at the playbook yet?"

"Oh, yes," Kim said.

"Me too," Pamela said. "You know, playing a witch is going to be fun. I'm the First Witch, you know." She cackled good-naturedly, "When shall we three meet again? In thunder, lightning, or in rain?"

"That's good," Kim said. Pamela seemed so happy. Surely she couldn't be the one sending those messages.

Rodney glanced at Kim. "Remember, you've got to really get under Lady Macbeth's skin. She's often played completely wrong. She's played as this one-dimensional evil demon who led poor old Macbeth astray, but she's more complex than that. And don't forget, he's not innocent either. The whole play hangs on us making Macbeth and his wife believable, Kim."

Kim nodded. Rodney had fierce, blue eyes, and his most common expression was a frown. He seemed really concerned that Kim would not do well in the role and it would reflect on him. Perhaps he'd be crazy enough to try to frighten her into dropping out so Pamela could take over.

Kim turned her attention to history as the teacher, Ms. Ives, came in. She was a young teacher with bright green eyes and red hair. There was a lot of gossip at Anthony High that Ms. Ives had a serious crush on Mr. Gabriel. But rumor had it that Mr. Gabriel didn't even know she existed. Kim had always noticed that when Mr. Gabriel walked past the open door, Ms. Ives seemed to lose her train of thought.

Kim thought Ms. Ives was a good teacher, and she felt sorry for her. It had to be hard to like someone very much who paid no attention to you at all. Mr. Gabriel was so focused on his drama classes that he had no time or interest in having a social life. Poor Ms. Ives, Kim thought.

"Everyone was building up armaments . . . there was a ferocious arms race, a stockpiling of weapons," Ms. Ives was saying. "It was inevitable that with so much firepower on both sides, a war would break out."

"War is such a stupid thing," Pamela commented. "I mean, we punish little kids for hitting each other, but when they are older and blow up other people, that makes them heroes. You'd think after all these years we would've learned to stop war."

"We have not yet learned to negotiate our differences," Ms. Ives said. "People have desires for land, power, and resources, and that's what leads to violence, to war." She was speaking with passion and enthusiasm when suddenly her voice faded. She was looking out the window.

Mr. Gabriel was walking by.

Pamela looked at Beth and winked. Both girls giggled.

....

As Kim and Arnetta were heading for lunch, Beth came from the opposite direction. Usually when she met Kim, she smiled, but this time she looked angry. She hurried by without saying a word.

"Arnetta," Kim gasped, "did you see that?"

"Yeah, she looked steamed. If looks could kill, you'd be a goner right now," Arnetta said.

"Oh, Arnetta, I bet she did want to play

Lady Macbeth, and now she's mad at me," Kim groaned.

"I don't know why she's mad at you," Arnetta said. "Mr. Gabriel made the choice."

All the rest of the afternoon, Kim wondered if Beth was behind the nasty messages. She had always seemed like a nice person, but like that old radio show said, nobody really knows what evil lurks in human minds.

After school, Kim saw Beth walking toward the parking area where the parents picked up students. "Beth," she called out, "may I talk to you a minute?"

Beth didn't turn. She kept on going toward the parking lot. Kim hurried to catch up to her. "Beth, what's the matter?" Kim asked when she was alongside the other girl.

Beth glared at Kim. "Like you don't know!"

"I don't know. You seem so angry with me, but I don't know why. Please tell me," Kim said.

"You are such a two-faced little sneak," Beth said bitterly.

"What are you talking about?" Kim asked.

"Look," Beth said, finally stopping and turning toward Kim. "I wasn't anxious to play Lady Macbeth. To tell you the truth, it's too much work. I was kind of relieved to get Lady Macduff. But you had to go all around the school gloating about how you beat me out of the role. You told everybody I was dying to play Lady Macbeth, even though I'm not very talented, and that Mr. Gabriel picked you because you are so talented."

Kim was shocked. "Beth, I never gloated about it. I never even talked about you not getting the role. Who told you I did that? It's all a complete lie!" Kim cried. Kim was terribly upset. She tried so hard to be kind to everyone. If her parents drilled one lesson into her mind and heart, it was to avoid hurting others by word or deed. Kim took that lesson very much to heart.

"Yeah, right," Beth snapped. "Well, somebody told me you were prancing all over school saying how disappointed I was to be playing Lady Macduff. I never wanted to be Lady Macbeth, but now that you've been such a creep about it, I hope you get laryngitis on opening night!"

"Beth, it's a lie," Kim said. "Somebody has told you a terrible lie just to make trouble. You must believe me. I'm not the kind of person who would say such things. That would be cruel and wicked, and I wouldn't do it."

"Don't waste your breath," Beth snapped. "The person who told me has no reason to lie."

"Who told you?" Kim asked.

Beth sneered. "Do you think I'd tell you? You'd just start spreading nasty lies about that person. You told everybody I was pouting and crying like a baby, and now all my friends are making fun of me. I feel like such a fool!"

"The person who told you those things about me is a liar," Kim said.

Beth turned and walked toward the parking lot. Kim turned and headed for the bus stop. Tears were in her eyes, but she refused to let them run down her face. She wiped her eyes.

Kim had always gotten along fine with Beth. Now they were bitter enemies. How could such a thing have happened? First the vile messages threatening Kim, and now somebody had lied about her to turn Beth against her. What was going on?

Kim had been happy when she was chosen to play Lady Macbeth. She thought that being in this play would be one of the high school memories she would cherish all her life. But ever since she had been chosen, it seemed as if a dark shadow had descended on her. It was like something wicked had come to life and was attacking her.

"Kim," Huong said as he approached her. "You look so sad. What's the matter? You aren't getting stage fright about playing Lady Macbeth, are you?"

"No, it's not that," Kim said. She told Huong everything that had happened, including Beth's accusation. "Huong, why is all this happening? It's like a spell has been cast upon me," Kim cried.

"I think somebody is trying to drive you from the play, Kim," Huong said.

"Arnetta thinks Pamela really wanted to play Lady Macbeth so she could spend all that time with Rodney. But Pamela is being really nice to me. I just don't understand it," Kim said.

"Maybe Pamela is a better actress than we think," Huong said. "Beth is her friend. She could have poisoned Beth against you."

Kim glanced across the campus to Pamela who was being picked up by her father. Pamela spotted Kim and waved warmly. She seemed to be smiling in her usual pleasant way.

3 KIM HAD NEVER dealt with a problem like this before. She was a good student, and she had a part-time job at a day care center. She did very well with the children. In fact, in everything Kim did, she excelled. When there was a problem, she met it head on and solved it. Last summer Huong and his parents wanted Kim to go with them on a trip to the Grand Canyon. But it conflicted with a computer class Kim really needed to have. When Kim told Huong she couldn't go on the trip he was hurt and a little angry. But after talking to him, Kim got Huong to understand and accept her decision.

But how could she deal with this, when she didn't know what it was? She knew someone was trying to hurt her, but who? And why?

When Kim got home, there was a letter for her on the table. Immediately, Kim got nervous. Usually she did not receive letters except from relatives in distant places.

"Mom, do you have any idea who this

letter might be from?" Kim called out to her mother, who was emptying the dishwasher.

"Let me see it. Hmm, the letter doesn't have a return address," her mother said, "but it seems to be personal. It's not junk mail. What's the matter? Do you think there's bad news in the letter? You look frightened, Kim."

"No, Mom," Kim said quickly. "I was uh . . . thinking of something else." Kim walked over to the sofa with the letter and opened it. The outside address had been typed and so was the note inside.

> "In the cauldron boil and bake,
> Hear my spell and faint and shake,
> Flee, o flee from Macbeth's wife,
> Flee, my child, for your very life."

Kim's mom saw how shaken she was, so she took the note from Kim's hands. "What is this nonsense, Kim?" she demanded.

"Oh, Mom, somebody at school is playing wicked tricks on me, and I don't know who it is," Kim said, her voice trembling.

"But you've never had an enemy in school," her mother said, fear on her face.

"What has happened to cause this?"

"I don't know, Mom," Kim said.

"Is it because of the play? Do you think another girl wanted to play the role they gave you?" her mother asked.

"There was just Pamela and Beth in the running for Lady Macbeth. Neither one seemed to want it very much," Kim said. "Maybe this is just a cruel person who enjoys playing tricks on people."

"But it is so frightening," her mother said.

Kim's father walked in the door, and he read the note. "Kim Hyun got this in the mail," her mother explained. "It is the third message she's gotten like this."

"Kim, this sounds like a threat," her father said, his eyes narrowing.

"I think it's a bad joke, Dad," Kim said. "I'm going to try to find out who's doing this."

"Maybe a boy is trying to get your attention, and this is how he's doing it," her mother said. "Boys do crazy things to get noticed by a girl they like."

"Yes, maybe," Kim said. Everybody at school knew that she and Huong were dating. But maybe a boy she had never noticed had a secret crush on her.

"Kim," her father said in a grave voice, "if somebody is so angry about you playing the role of Lady Macbeth in the play that they would harm you, then you must drop out at once. The play is not worth risking your life!"

"I know, Dad, but I really don't think it's that serious," Kim said.

"You never know what some angry person might do," her father insisted, reacting just as Kim feared he would, suspecting the worse. "You are our precious daughter. We could not bear it if harm came to you. Excelling in a play is not worth taking risks."

"I know, Dad," Kim said, "but I'm sure it's just someone's idea of a joke. I told my teacher, Mr. Gabriel, about it, and he thought some clown was behind it."

Just then, the phone rang. All three family members grew quiet. Kim picked up the phone and said in a small voice, "Yes?"

"Kim, this is Tyler," Tyler Kern said.

Kim let out a huge sigh of relief. "Oh, hi, Tyler," she said.

"I'm going over the playbook, Kim, and I'm kind of confused on this Macduff guy. I wonder if we could maybe study together for an hour after school tomorrow . . . maybe at my house? I live just across the street from Anthony High. Then, when we're done, I could drive you home," Tyler said. "You're so good at this kind of stuff . . . "

"Just a minute, Tyler. I'll ask my parents," Kim said. "Hey, Mom, Tyler Kern, that new student, is having trouble with his character, and he asked me to help him. He's a senior, and he has a car, so he'll drive me home afterward. He's a real careful driver, Mom."

Her mother thought for a moment, then she smiled. "Oh, yes. I met Mrs. Kern, Tyler's mother, at the open house. We both baked chocolate chip cookies. I'm sure it will be fine, Kim," she said.

....

The next day in history class, Kim turned in her report early. It was a big relief to get it off her mind. Now she could concentrate on *Macbeth*.

"Oh, my," Ms. Ives said, "a report coming in already! That's excellent, Kim. It gives me more time to grade these reports if you don't all wait until the last minute."

Rodney glanced over at Kim and muttered, "It must be wonderful to be such a genius that you get everything done so far ahead of time."

"I'm not a genius," Kim said. "I just push myself."

Ms. Ives was setting up to show a movie about World War I when Pamela leaned across the aisle. "Kim, I tried on my witch's costume, and it was so cool!" She laughed and deepened her voice, "In the cauldron boil and bake!"

Kim turned ice-cold. Those were the opening words in the last threatening message! And with her voice deepened, Pamela sounded just like that voice on the phone! Of course it was probably just a coincidence. Pamela was studying her dialogue for *Macbeth*, so naturally she would know those lines.

Kim looked at Pamela and asked, "Did you want to play Lady Macbeth, Pamela?"

Pamela shrugged and said, "Well, yeah,

it would have been nice. But I'll have fun anyway playing the First Witch. It's no big deal."

"Sometimes I feel bad that I got the part, and you didn't," Kim said, fishing for some clue. She wanted to give Pamela an opportunity to show her true feelings. If there was hatred or bitterness in Pamela's eyes, Kim thought they might show themselves.

But Pamela's sunny smile remained. "I'll tell you one thing, Kim," she said in a half-serious voice, "just because you'll be spending so much time with my boyfriend, don't get any ideas. He's mine."

"Yes," Rodney said sarcastically, "Kim and I will be playing that sweet couple. How romantic when all they do is talk about murder! What a pair. No Romeo and Juliet here."

Pamela and Kim both laughed. Kim glanced around the classroom for a few seconds before Ms. Ives dimmed the lights. Kim scanned the faces of the boys in the room, searching for someone who might be looking at her in an unhealthy way. Some secret admirer, who was desperately trying to get her attention by unsettling her mind.

Kim didn't see anybody who fit the description. But maybe the boy was in one of her other classes at Anthony High.

Kim was beautiful with golden skin and large, expressive eyes. She was tall and slim. When she was a freshman she went to a football game with a boy she hardly knew, and he said, "Kim, you are the most perfect girl I have ever seen." Kim had laughed. She didn't feel so perfect.

But that boy had treated her like a princess. Maybe he was still at Anthony High. Kim had forgotten him, but maybe he had not forgotten her.

4 "HEY, TYLER," Kim said after he greeted her at the Kerns' door.

"Hey, come on in."

The two walked into the den, and Tyler got his playbook out. "You know, it's hard to get under Macduff's skin because he seems like such a hero. Macbeth is the power-hungry evil one, but Macduff . . . "

Kim smiled. "Macbeth is much more complex than that. He has done these terrible things, but he is haunted by them, so that means he has a conscience," she said.

"What do you think drove him to murder, Kim? You think his wife put all this pressure on him?" Tyler asked.

"My character, yes," Kim said. "She did push him. But then he plans to commit another murder on his own, so there was darkness inside him."

"You've got it all figured out, haven't you?" Tyler said. "You're really smart."

"No, I just read a lot. I like to know things," Kim said.

"Kim, do you think just anybody could be driven to . . . doing some awful thing . . . like maybe even killing somebody? If the right pressures were there, do you think a . . . normal person could be driven to do something extreme?" Tyler asked.

"I don't know," Kim said. "Maybe."

"I'm interested in psychology," Tyler said. "When I finish high school I think I'll major in that in college."

"Oh, that's good," Kim said. "You can help people with their problems."

Tyler glanced toward the kitchen where his mother was making cookies. She was taking them from the oven. Whenever Tyler had a friend over, his mother baked fresh cookies and served them on a silver tray with coffee or milk. Tyler lowered his voice to make sure his mother couldn't hear. "My dad, he was under so much pressure at his job that he had a nervous breakdown."

"Oh, that's very sad," Kim said, surprised at the sudden change of subject. When Tyler and his mother had moved into the neighborhood last summer, Kim had assumed the father and husband was either dead or divorced. "Were the doctors able to help your father?" Kim asked.

"No," Tyler said. "They weren't any good. Here was this poor guy, just totally out of whack mentally, and they couldn't do anything."

"That's terrible," Kim said, beginning to understand why Tyler wanted to be a psychologist. He wanted to help people in a way his father was not helped.

Mrs. Kern brought the cookies and drinks. "Have as many as you like, dear," she told Kim. Mrs. Kern was a slender, weary-looking woman who looked much older than she probably was.

"Thanks, Mom," Tyler said, but he seemed a little embarrassed by the ritual. It seemed he would have preferred his mother staying out of the way when he had somebody over. When his mother disappeared back into the kitchen Tyler grinned at Kim. "My mom is kind of old fashioned. She always thinks she has to play hostess when somebody comes over even for a few minutes."

"I think it's very sweet," Kim said. "My mother is the same way."

They spent some time talking about

Macduff and how Tyler could humanize him so he wasn't just a perfect hero. Kim liked Tyler. He was easy to talk to, and because of that she made the decision to share the threatening notes she had received with him.

"Look, this one came in the mail," Kim said, as she revealed the latest threat.

Tyler read the note that concluded, "Flee, my child, for your very life."

"Wow, somebody's got it in for you, Kim," Tyler said. "I guess it must be somebody in the cast of *Macbeth*."

"I can't believe there's anybody there who'd want to play such mean tricks on me," Kim said.

"Could be they just want to mess with your head, Kim. Just yank your chain, you know?" Tyler said.

"Well, I'm very strong," Kim said resolutely. "I'm not going to let anybody spoil this wonderful chance that came my way."

"Good for you, Kim," Tyler said. "That's the spirit. And listen, you've really helped me a lot today. I think I understand Macduff a lot better."

The two walked down the driveway to Tyler's car. "Thanks for offering to drive me home, Tyler. It gets dark so early these days, and who knows who's out there on the streets."

Kim got in Tyler's car, and he pulled into the street. "You're really a pretty girl, Kim," Tyler said.

"Thank you," Kim said, surprised by the comment. She had seen Tyler with several pretty girls but had never thought he had much interest in her.

Kim told Tyler where she lived. "I usually just take the bus home. I live about three miles from the school."

"That's a hassle, the bus," Tyler said.

"Oh, I don't mind. I usually find a friend to talk to on the way, so the time goes very fast," Kim said.

"Uh, Kim, it's none of my business, but I just wondered, have you always dated Huong Lam?" Tyler asked.

"Our families have been close for generations back in Vietnam, and Huong and I were both born in this neighborhood. We have been friends forever, but we just started dating when I started my junior year and he started his senior year," Kim said. "We have great fun together. He is such a happy person. That means a lot to me. I can get down sometimes, but he is always looking for the funny side of everything. He can always lift my spirits."

"Is Huong happy about you taking on Lady Macbeth?" Tyler asked.

"Oh, sure," Kim said. "He's happy for me, because he knows how much I wanted it."

"Yeah, but how will you two find time to spend together?" Tyler asked.

"Well, sure, I'll be busy with rehearsals and everything, but Huong understands. I understand when he has to practice for tennis," Kim said.

"Huong isn't as happy as you think about you being in the play, Kim," Tyler said suddenly.

Kim stared at Tyler. "What makes you say that?"

"We have Algebra II together, and the other day he was telling some of us that he was losing his girlfriend to some stupid play," Tyler said.

"Oh," Kim said, "he was only joking. Huong jokes all the time. He would never have said that seriously."

"He sure looked serious to me," Tyler insisted. "But I guess I never should have mentioned it. Me and my big mouth. I don't want to make trouble between you guys."

"It's all right," Kim said. "My house is the one on the corner, Tyler."

After Tyler pulled into the driveway he said, "Thanks a lot for helping me with Macduff, Kim."

"Sure. Thanks for the ride," Kim said.

As Kim climbed out of the car and walked to her door, she thought about Huong Lam. She and Huong had been close for many years. For a long time he was like a big brother. But then Kim and Huong decided it was more than that, and they began dating each other.

It bothered Kim that Huong had made that joke about losing his girlfriend to the play. Maybe he did feel some resentment about how busy Kim would be.

When Kim got to her room, she called Huong.

"I worked with Tyler Kern on the play this afternoon," she said. "He was feeling unsure about how to play Macduff."

"Oh, that was nice of you," Huong said.

"There will be a lot of work over the next few weeks, Huong. We will be very busy with the play. I hope you don't mind too much. I don't want you to feel neglected," Kim said, hoping she was inviting Huong to express his true feelings, even bad feelings.

"I understand that, Kim. We talked about it. It will all be worth it when I see my girl up there emoting on the stage. I've called and e-mailed cousins and old friends, and they're all coming to see *Macbeth*. I'm going to be so proud of you. Imagine, my girl, starring in the first production of a Shakespeare play ever done at our school," Huong said.

"I'm glad you feel like that, Huong," Kim said.

There was a brief silence at the other end of the line. "Kim, you sound weird. Is something wrong?" he asked.

"No . . . but, somebody told me they overheard you sort of complaining about me spending so much time on the play. I thought maybe you were afraid to tell me your true feelings," Kim said.

"Does that sound like me?" Huong asked.

"No," Kim admitted. "We've always been very honest with each other."

"And I'll always be that way. Sure, I'm going to miss us being together as much as we usually are, but I know it's just for a few weeks. It'll be a great thing, so don't worry about it," Huong said.

After Kim hung up the phone, she still felt uneasy. Lately she had been feeling uneasy about everything, and that was unusual for her. She was usually happy and secure. She began her math homework, but it was hard to concentrate. When she went into the living room and watched a sitcom with Sham, her brother was laughing his head off, but Kim didn't get it. She wasn't in the mood for it.

....

At lunch the next day, Kim talked to Arnetta about how she felt. "I got another of those stupid threatening notes, Arnetta. It came in the mail this time," Kim said, letting Arnetta read it.

"You need to go to Mr. Gabriel and talk to him again," Arnetta said.

"He just brushed it off the first time. I hate to bother him. He's got so much work and pressure to get *Macbeth* ready," Kim said.

"Kim, you've got to tell the man. It's not a joke when all these threats are coming at you. Somebody is messing with your mind, and you've got to find out who and why. It's not just you. The whole play is at stake. Mr. Gabriel has the right to know," Arnetta said.

Kim nodded. "You're right. I'll talk to him after school."

After her last class that day, Kim walked toward the drama room. Mr. Gabriel would be in there alone, going over playbooks and other details. He was always in his room long after the last classes ended.

Kim was embarrassed to be bothering Mr. Gabriel with her problem. The teacher would probably regret that he had given the role of Lady Macbeth to her.

5 MR. GABRIEL LOOKED UP when Kim came in. "Oh, hi, Kim."

Kim tried to start the conversation on a positive note so she said, "Tyler and I are working on our characters so that we can get all the complex personalities down."

"Excellent," Mr. Gabriel said. "I'm glad you dropped in, Kim. There was something I wanted to talk to you about."

"Yes?"

"I'm sure there's nothing to it, but a third party told me there's some personality conflict going on between you and Beth Skinner. Some nonsense about your friends wanting to beat her up or something. I don't know where these stupid rumors get started. Naturally, I didn't believe any of it, but I just wanted to touch base with you. This play is too important to me to let anything distract us. I've been trying to get Anthony High to tackle a play by Shakespeare for five years, and now that it's finally happening, I absolutely refuse to let anything get in the way," Mr. Gabriel said.

Kim was devastated. She wanted to tell Mr. Gabriel about Beth's confrontation. But that would just confirm his fears that some sort of catfight was going on in the cast of *Macbeth*. He wouldn't be interested in all the gory details. All he cared about was the play. "No, it's not true," Kim said quietly. "We have always gotten along fine."

"Good. I thought the rumor was baseless," Mr. Gabriel said. "I expect complete professionalism from everyone here. That's the only way we can get a great play performed. Now, what did you want to see me about?"

"Uh . . . I wanted to make sure I had the date for our first rehearsal," Kim lied. She was not about to bring up the distressing subject of the threatening notes she was getting. She would have to deal with them herself.

"Oh. Here's a copy of our schedule," he said, handing her the computer printout.

Kim left the classroom. As she walked down the hall, she spotted Ms. Ives standing there. She was looking in the direction of the drama room. Obviously, she was waiting for Mr. Gabriel, hoping he would emerge from the room so she could accidentally-on-purpose run into him.

When their eyes met, Ms. Ives seemed to Kim to be a little embarrassed. "Does Mr. Gabriel seem very busy?" she asked Kim. "I need to see him about scheduling in the auditorium."

"He's going over the playbooks for *Macbeth*," Kim said.

"Yes, of course," Ms. Ives said. She seemed to stare at Kim, almost as if it had crossed her mind that this beautiful teenager was consuming Mr. Gabriel's attention.

"Well, see you tomorrow, Ms. Ives."

There was still time for Kim to catch the bus, so she hurried. She ran across the campus to the bus stop in front of the school. She noticed Pamela there waiting for the bus too.

"Hi, Kim," Pamela sang out in a friendly voice.

"Hi, Pamela," Kim answered.

Pamela giggled. "Here I was worried that you and Rodney would be spending so much time together that maybe you'd fall in love with him and he'd forget about me. But you have bigger fish to fry, don't you?" she asked.

"What do you mean, Pam?" Kim asked.

"Come on, admit it, Kim. You've got a major crush on Damian Gabriel," Pamela said.

"No, I haven't. I respect him very much as a good drama teacher, but I haven't got a crush on him," Kim said.

"Oh, come on. A little bird told me you hang around his room every chance you get," Pamela laughed. "This little bird told me that you're crazy about Mr. Gabriel. Don't be ashamed of it, Kim. We're all a little bit in love with him. Let's face it—he's cute!"

Kim smiled. But the truth was she did not have the least bit of a crush on Mr. Gabriel.

Kim was scheduled to work at the day care center after school that day. It was just two blocks from her house. She got off the bus at her house, and then walked the two blocks north to the center. Kim's class consisted of five three- to six-year-old children, and she worked on art and music projects with them. Today they were going to begin an origami project.

"We'll make whales today," Kim told the children.

"A whale is too big," a little girl insisted. She spread her arms as wide as she could and said, "A whale is this big."

Kim smiled. "Our whales will be little. Baby whales."

Kim began helping the little hands shape the purple and white squares with simple folds.

Dusk came quickly and while Kim was absorbed in folding the origami, the sun went down. The lights were bright in the room, so she never noticed.

The little purple and white whales were lined up on the worktable, their tailfins thrust up.

"Now we draw eyes and a mouth on our whales with black markers," Kim said. When it was done, the children squealed with delight at their masterpieces.

Ms. Brosner, the director of the day care center, had been standing in the doorway watching the lesson. She beamed. After

Kim helped the children put their names on the whales so they could take them home and show them to their parents, Ms. Brosner came into the room.

"Kim, you are so good with the children. I wish we could have you here full time," she said.

"Thank you. I love working here," Kim said.

"Kim," one of the little boys yelled suddenly, as he stared up at the window. "Is that ori . . . ori . . . "

"Origami," Kim said, following his finger to the window. Something was hanging on the outside of the window, something strange.

"Is that origami?" the boy asked again.

Kim left the room and went outside. Dangling from a nail above the window was a paper skeleton, the kind they sell around Halloween. But Halloween had already passed.

"What's that? Is that a skeleton?" the boy asked after Kim brought it inside.

"Yes," Kim said with a smile. "It was left over from Halloween." Her heart was pounding, but she kept a smile on her face for the sake of the child.

When Kim was alone with Ms. Brosner, the woman asked, "Who would hang that ugly thing outside the window of a day care center? What's the matter with people?"

"I guess it was somebody's idea of a joke," Kim said in a faltering voice. "Like maybe junior high boys or something."

Kim hoped that Ms. Brosner wouldn't see the note dangling from the skeleton, but she noticed it. "Look, a note is taped to the skeleton's ribs," Ms. Brosner said.

Kim felt the room darken. She didn't want to read the contents of the note. She wanted to throw it out and go home and pretend none of this was happening.

But Ms. Brosner said, "How odd . . . it sounds like some verse . . . something from Shakespeare . . .

> Gall of goat and slips of yew,
> My greatest spell should trouble you.
> Play not the tyrant's bloody queen,
> Or you shall be quite soon unseen."

Ms. Brosner looked at Kim in bewilderment. "Have you any idea what this is all about?"

"I was chosen to play Lady Macbeth in a school play, and ever since then I've been getting these messages," Kim said.

"Oh, my. I'm afraid jealousy is rearing its ugly head. I'll bet another girl had her heart set on the part," Ms. Brosner said.

Kim always walked the two blocks home after she finished working at the day care center. Kim was a good brisk walker, and she was usually home in just a few minutes. Still, she was nervous tonight as she had never been before.

Kim sometimes thought Beth Skinner was behind the notes, but at other times she was sure it was somebody else, maybe someone she didn't even know. That was very frightening.

Kim wore her school backpack, and it felt heavier than usual because of the stress. She kept glancing behind her to make sure no one was following her. She thought about the freshman boy who took her to the football game, and once again she tried to remember his name. He had made such a small impression on her, but maybe she had made a lasting impression on him . . .

Halfway home, as Kim looked back, she saw a dark figure coming behind her. It was not unusual that someone would be walking home from work on this street. Usually Kim paid no attention to it. Stores were closing. Clerks and merchants were going home. But Kim got a nervous chill when she looked back, and noticed that the dark figure was gaining on her. It looked like a man or a very tall boy.

Kim was passing a little house where, as a junior high student, she used to work. An elderly lady lived there, and Kim used to make money pulling weeds and mowing her lawn. Impulsively, Kim hurried up the flower-lined walk and rang the doorbell.

"Why, Kim," the white-haired lady said when she opened the door, "how nice to see you. My, you have grown. It's been several years, hasn't it?"

"Yes," Kim said, though it had only been a year since Kim had stopped by to clear overgrown vines from the yard.

"Come on in, dear," the woman said.

Kim sat in the parlor with a gray cat purring at her heels and listened to the woman talk about her children and grandchildren. Kim's mind was outside, in the darkness. She wondered if whoever was following her had gone past the house. Kim told the woman about being in *Macbeth* at school, and then Kim promised to come by again as soon as she could.

When Kim stepped outside, she didn't see anybody. She wasn't far from her house. If she walked very fast, she should be home in just a few minutes.

Thick hedges edged the yards. Kim couldn't help but think that someone might be hiding behind one. Kim looked straight ahead, fearful that if she looked to her right where the hedges cast their shadows in the moonlight, she would see him.

Kim saw her house in the distance. Just a few seconds, and she'd be home. She glanced back.

He was coming again. Or someone was coming.

Kim's heart began to pound.

KIM BROKE INTO A RUN. She was at her own driveway when she got the courage to look back.

There was no one there.

Kim's legs ached, and she was breathless. The person who had been following her probably had nothing to do with her. It was just somebody on their way home. Kim's panic had created a monster when there was no monster.

"What is happening to me?" Kim groaned to herself.

Before she had the chance to go in the house, Kim spotted her father in the backyard looking through the telescope. He smiled and waved when he saw Kim. "Venus is beautiful tonight. Come and look," he said.

Usually Kim loved to see heavenly sights through her father's telescope, but now she was too exhausted and upset to appreciate anything. "I think I'll just go inside," she said.

"Kim Hyun," her father said, "is everything all right?"

"It's been a long day," Kim said. "I worked very hard with the children at the day care center."

Kim went to her room and put on some classical music to help her relax. She liked all kinds of music, including pop rock, but now she needed soothing music. Tomorrow was the first rehearsal for *Macbeth*. For the first time since this had all started, Kim wondered if she was up to it. It crossed her mind that maybe she should drop out, but she quickly banished the thought.

....

The next day after school, everybody met in the auditorium. Kim knew there were a lot of kids involved, but she had no idea there were this many. In addition to the cast there were students working on sets, lighting, publicity, makeup, programs, and costumes.

The primary actors gathered in one corner of the auditorium and began working on their scenes. Rodney seemed very tense, like his life depended on everything going well.

"Kim," he snapped, "where's your playbook? We're doing Act I, scene 5."

Kim turned to the chair she had been sitting on. She had set her playbook down when she got up. "It's gone!" she cried. "It was right here a few minutes ago!" Kim looked around frantically. "I've lost my playbook. It has my name on it. Will everyone check and see if they picked up my book by mistake?"

Beth looked at Kim and sneered. Maybe she had snatched it up and hidden it out of spite! Tyler, who was working on another scene, came over to help Kim search.

Rodney stood there rolling his eyes. "Mr. Gabriel, Kim has managed to lose her playbook, and we haven't even started rehearsal. Is that a bad omen or what?" he said.

Mr. Gabriel seemed annoyed too. Kim was getting a splitting headache. "We can't have this," Mr. Gabriel said as he brought another playbook for her to use. "People, please take care of your things. We can't be wasting precious time with distractions!"

"Oh, grand," Rodney said. "Does this mean that we can finally rehearse?"

Kim glared at the good-looking boy. He was obnoxious most of the time, and the rest of the time he was just irritating. A real downside of winning the role of Lady Macbeth was spending time with Rodney.

Kim briefly went off stage and then entered, a letter in her hand. "They met me in the day of success," she began.

"No, no, no," Mr. Gabriel said, "You sound like you're reading a laundry list. You are supposed to be triumphant! You have great news. You have read a letter predicting that your husband shall be king!"

Rodney rolled his eyes again and folded his arms in disgust. Kim could tell right from the start that he wasn't thrilled that she had gotten the role of Lady Macbeth. He wanted his girlfriend, Pamela, to get the part. For a terrible second, Kim wondered if Rodney were behind the campaign of harassment against her.

Kim made her entrance a second time and began speaking. This time Mr. Gabriel said, "Good! Good! Light-years better. Keep it at that level." Then Mr. Gabriel hurried over to watch the witches who were rehearsing Act I, scene 1.

When Rodney's turn to speak came, his chest puffed out like a peacock. "Great Glamis! Worthy Cawdor," he bellowed. Kim grudgingly had to admit that he was a very good actor, especially for a 17-year-old boy. He seemed much older. He was a credible Macbeth. He had already played the lead in three other plays and gotten rave reviews.

Rodney turned toward Kim, and his piercing eyes on her made her nervous. He held out his hands to her. "My dearest love! Duncan comes here tonight!" he said.

"And when goes hence?" Kim asked.

Rodney rolled his eyes again. "More feeling, Kim! Not so wimpy! Lady Macbeth was not a wimp. Remember, she was about to goad Macbeth into bloody murder. This was a woman to be reckoned with. The 'fiend like queen,' " he cried.

Kim tried again. After two hours of rehearsal, Kim felt like she had been dragged through the streets by galloping horses. Rodney's constant criticism and Mr. Gabriel's scolding caused Kim to consider scrapping the entire project.

But, stubbornly, Kim refused to do that. Her parents had taught her to never give up. Kim knew she could be a good Lady Macbeth, and she just had to weather the storm.

As Kim was walking from the auditorium, Tyler came up beside her. "You look beat," he said.

"Yeah, I am," Kim admitted.

"How are you getting home?" Tyler asked.

"My dad is picking me up," Kim said. "I called him on my cell phone."

"After this, let me drive you home after rehearsals," Tyler offered. "Wouldn't be any trouble."

"Thanks, Tyler," Kim said. "I need all the help I can get!"

At that moment Kim heard Mr. Gabriel's voice. "Kim!"

Mr. Gabriel reached Kim and Tyler. "Good job tonight, Tyler," he said. "You're a good Macduff." Then he turned to Kim. "Don't take all that happened tonight to heart, Kim. You were very good for someone with your limited experience. I'm very brutal in the early rehearsals, but, as time goes by,

I get more civilized." A smile cracked his dark face. "I knew what I was doing when I chose you for Lady Macbeth. You'll do just fine."

"Thank you, Mr. Gabriel," Kim said. "I was really nervous. I'll do a lot better next time."

Mr. Gabriel smiled and nodded, then hurried off. Kim felt much better as she walked toward her father's car.

"How was the rehearsal?" her father asked as they rolled from the curb.

"Really hard and stressful, but good," Kim said.

"Well, it's going to be a lot of work, but if you are sure you want to do it, then you will succeed," her father said.

"It'll be so much fun. Last year I had a tiny part in *Arms and the Man*, and I just loved it. It was exciting being part of the cast and growing together like a family," Kim said.

"Well, before I left home to come get you, a bouquet of flowers came to the house addressed to you. I guess you've impressed somebody, because they're already sending you flowers," her father said. "Maybe your teacher, Mr. Gabriel, sent them."

"Mr. Gabriel wouldn't do something like that," Kim said. She thought of Huong and smiled. He knew how nervous she was about the rehearsal, especially after getting those threatening messages. Huong must have sent the flowers! Kim hoped Huong didn't spend a lot of money on them. He came from a big family and money was short.

It would be just like Huong to blow money on a lavish bouquet just to cheer Kim up.

"Did you see who the flowers were from, Dad?" Kim asked.

"No. The note must be inside. It's a very big box though. You said this boy, Rodney Ormsley, is playing Macbeth. Since you are playing Lady Macbeth, maybe he sent you the flowers to make you feel more comfortable," her father said.

Kim laughed. "Rodney? Oh, no way. He's got about as much sentimentality as a rock! All he thinks about is himself. If he ever sent flowers, it would be to himself!"

Her father laughed as they pulled into their driveway.

The laughter faded as soon as they saw Sham and his mother on the front lawn with the pretty white box. They looked really upset.

"What's going on?" Kim's father asked.

"The box started smelling really bad, and we had to get it out of the house," Sham said.

Kim began to turn numb. Even in the open air, she smelled it too.

"I thought it was a bouquet of flowers," Sham continued, "but there's something else in there!"

Kim stood there for a few seconds. Then she lifted the cover of the box.

"Ewwwww," Kim cried, "it's garbage! It's nothing but smelly old garbage with ants on it!"

A note was stuck inside the box, but Kim did not want to open it.

7 KIM GINGERLY PICKED UP the
note. It was unsigned. She did not
really expect otherwise. They were
all unsigned. When Kim saw the horrified
look on her mother's face, she forced a
smile to her own ashen face. "Oh, it's from
some jerk in biology. He's always doing
stupid stuff like this," Kim lied, just so her
parents would not be alarmed.

"I've never heard of such a disgusting
thing," her mother said.

"Oh, he's always doing crazy stuff. He's
sort of like a mad scientist," Kim said.

"Well, throw the horrid thing in the
trash," her mother said, "and Kim, you tell
that boy that his sick sense of humor is not
appreciated."

Kim hurried to her room with the note
and forced herself to open it. She knew
what it was. It was another one of those
vile messages, but she didn't dare let her
parents know. They would be so frightened
they wouldn't let her remain in the play.
Kim was trembling as she read,

"Thrice the brinded cat has mewed,
Now the horror will be brewed,
You listened not, you closed your ears,
Now await the bitter tears."

Kim sank back in the chair, the note fluttering to the floor.

It had to be Beth, Kim thought. Beth must have stolen Kim's playbook too, just to mess with her mind.

....

At school on Monday morning, Kim waited for Beth to walk in the doors of Anthony High. As Beth approached, Kim stepped into her path. "Hey, we've got to talk. You have to stop this horrible campaign against me," Kim said.

"What are you talking about?" Beth said, laughing sharply. "You're the one who went all over the school ridiculing! You hurt me. I never did anything to you!"

"Look," Kim said, thrusting the latest note at Beth. "I got this in a box filled with garbage. This is the fifth note I've gotten like this. I think you're sending them, Beth. Just as a way to get even with me for something I never did!"

"You are sick!" Beth cried. "I've never seen this note before. You're probably making them up and sending them to yourself just so you can play the poor little persecuted actress!"

"Beth, I never gloated about winning the role of Lady Macbeth. Whoever told you I did is a liar," Kim insisted. "Can't we settle this?"

"Just get out of my way," Beth snapped. "I'm late for class."

Kim watched the other girl disappear into a classroom. All day, until lunchtime, Kim couldn't think of anything but the box of garbage and the latest horrible note. Then, just before lunch, Tyler came along. "You eating lunch in the cafeteria?" he asked.

"No. I brought some yogurt. I think I'll just find a shady spot to eat," Kim said.

"Mind some company?" Tyler asked.

"That'd be nice," Kim said.

They walked to a grassy knoll and sat down under the spreading branches of a mulberry tree.

"Kim, I need to talk to you, and I'm kind of dreading it," Tyler began.

Kim was surprised. Tyler looked so serious that it frightened her. "What is it? What's the matter?" she asked.

"It's going to upset you, Kim," Tyler warned.

"Just tell me," Kim pleaded.

"Well, you know, we've got a lot of different kinds of kids here, and we all get along okay most of the time. But that doesn't mean there's not some, you know, prejudice," Tyler said. "I mean, I'm white, and I don't feel like that, but . . . "

"Tyler, just say what you have to say," Kim said.

"Well, some of the kids in drama class don't like the idea of a Vietnamese girl playing Lady Macbeth," Tyler said. "I was always cool with it, and I think you'll be great. But I've heard a lot of nasty stuff. Like, it spoils the play when somebody so different is playing a major role," Tyler said.

"Oh," Kim said. "I never gave that a thought. Of course the characters are mostly English in Shakespeare's plays. But there are so many African American, Hispanic, and Asian kids in our cast. I didn't think anybody noticed anymore."

"Well," Tyler said, "right after you were chosen, a bunch of us got together to talk about the play. And somebody brought up your race, and then some of the others chimed in. I said it didn't make any difference, and you'll have everybody believing you're Lady Macbeth by the end of scene 5."

Kim felt very sad. She had never felt any prejudice against her. Her best friend, Arnetta, was African American, and she had friends from every race and ethnic group. "Tyler, who is it that is upset with me playing Lady Macbeth?" Kim asked.

"Well, pretty much everybody but me and a couple of others," Tyler said.

"Rodney?" Kim asked. She had felt his hostility, but she never thought it was based on her being Vietnamese. He was mean and arrogant to everybody. She hadn't expected him to treat her any differently.

"Oh, yeah," Tyler said. "Especially him. He really thought Pamela should be Lady Macbeth. He said the chemistry was right there. He said it is all wrong between you and him."

"Oh," Kim said, her heart sinking. "Pamela feels that way too?"

"Yeah," Tyler said, "and Beth Skinner . . . the kids playing minor roles . . . some of them don't care, but all the important members of the cast feel about the same."

"Tyler, do you think this is why I'm getting those nasty messages?" Kim asked.

"I'm afraid so. It's sort of a group project," Tyler said.

Kim felt so bad she could not eat more than one fourth of her yogurt. "Tyler, in all the time I've been here at school, everybody has been nice to me," she said.

"Yeah, well, it's not cool to admit you've got these bigoted feelings. Kids try to cover them up. Except when they're with people who feel the same way," Tyler said.

Kim nodded, fighting back tears.

"I know where you're coming from, Kim," Tyler said. "I never told you before exactly what happened to my dad, but it was something like this. The people he worked with started a campaign of harassment against him to drive him from a project he was working on. He wasn't a different race, but he was just the kind of guy they didn't want around. He was a brilliant engineer, and he wouldn't stand for the shoddy work the others were doing, so they had to get rid of him."

Kim remembered the day she went to Tyler's house and how Tyler had referred to his father's sad fate. But he hadn't gone into detail.

"He was so much better than anybody else that they started to undermine him," Tyler said, his face in pain. "They launched this ugly little whispering campaign against him. Sort of what's happening to you, Kim, but more clever. They messed with his computer. They'd all get together and try to make it look like he was losing it . . . and in the end . . . in the end they got him."

"That's terrible, Tyler," Kim said.

"Yeah. It ruined us. We lost our house, the car. We had to move. Dad . . . he kind of snapped at the office . . . it was all because of what they'd done to him. Anybody else would have done the same thing. I mean, everybody's got a breaking point, right?" Tyler said. He was very pale now. He was clasping and unclasping his hands.

"Is your father still alive?" Kim asked.

"Yeah, if you can call that being alive," Tyler said. He reached out and impulsively took Kim's hand. "You know what you're feeling now? All stressed and everything? That's how he felt. They just kept coming at him until they broke him."

"I understand, Tyler. I'm very sorry," Kim said.

"So what are you going to do about your problem, Kim? Now that you know how they all feel, what are you going to do?" Tyler asked.

"Well, I'm not sleeping so well, and I'm not eating well, and I'm nervous. But still I'm not letting them push me out of the play. Mr. Gabriel stands behind me, supporting me. I'm not going to let him down. If I get out of the play now because of those cruel people, then evil has won. When my grandparents were coming to America, they had five children and only one, my father, survived. They continued the trip. They were strong, and I must be strong too. I must be strong to honor them. To honor the aunts and uncles who died," Kim said.

The bell rang, and Kim said good-bye to

Tyler and headed for her next class, math. Rodney was in that class. Kim did not know how she would be able to even look at him now. She had never liked him, but at least she had respected him. Now she didn't even respect him, and that made her sad.

8 IT WAS SO HARD for Kim to know the truth and to try to pretend that things were just the same. During math class, Rodney didn't hear the page number of the homework assignment so he leaned over toward Kim. "What page did he say?"

"Page 47," Kim said, staring straight ahead.

"Are you all right?" Rodney demanded. "You look weird. We have a rehearsal this afternoon, you know. I hope you're not sick. That's all we need."

"I'm fine," Kim said.

"It's scene 7," Rodney said. "We're getting to the heart of the play. The plot thickens. You've got some powerful dialogue. I hope you've gone over it."

"Yes," Kim said. How could he be such a hypocrite? How could he be acting as if they were both working for the good of the play, when he was working behind the scenes to frighten Kim out of her role?

By sheer force of will, Kim put everything

but the play out of her mind during the rehearsal. She faced Rodney in scene 7 and spoke her lines with vigor.

"But screw your courage to the sticking place!" Lady Macbeth was beginning to convince Macbeth how he would kill Duncan and secure the throne.

Rodney did not roll his eyes in frustration as much as he did before. He delivered his own lines powerfully, and Mr. Gabriel, who stood nearby to observe, did something he rarely did. He applauded both Kim and Rodney for the scene.

Kim would have been flushed with total happiness if she didn't know how so many in the cast felt about her. Now, as she walked with Tyler to his car after rehearsal, her heart ached.

"How did your rehearsal go?" she asked Tyler.

"It was good," Tyler said, "but I'm worried about you."

"I'll be okay. I'm just amazed how Rodney can act like nothing is wrong when he's trying to get rid of me," Kim said.

"He's a really good actor, I guess," Tyler said.

"I guess so," Kim said.

"Want to stop for pizza or anything?" Tyler asked.

"No, thank you. I just want to go home," Kim said.

As they drove, Tyler said, "Have you told your parents about the problem?"

"No. It would break my parents' hearts to know how other kids feel about me. They love America so much. They fly a big flag all the time," Kim said.

"Yeah," Tyler said, "it's best if you keep it from them. What about Huong?"

"I told Huong about the messages," Kim said.

"Huong is kind of a hothead. I'd be careful telling him," Tyler said. "He might haul off and attack some of those people in the cast."

"Huong is not a violent person," Kim said. "He's very gentle."

"You never know, Kim. He sort of reminds me of my father. Real quiet and smart, but when just the right buttons are pushed, look out," Tyler said.

After Kim got home, she called the only person she could pour her heart out to,

Arnetta. "I found out something horrible today, Arnetta," Kim said, telling her the whole story.

"I just can't believe that," Arnetta said.

"But it's true," Kim said. "It explains all those vile notes, and the garbage in the flower box, the skeleton outside the day care window . . . They want me out of the play, because they think a Vietnamese girl playing Lady Macbeth will ruin it."

"Kim, you have got to confront those creeps," Arnetta said. "There is no other way. You go and tell them what you know, and demand they explain themselves. Get it out in the open."

"Arnetta, they'll just deny everything. They won't admit what they really feel," Kim said, "and then it'll be impossible to work with them. As long as they don't know that I know, I can act fairly normal. But when it's all out in the open, I can't stay in the play."

After Kim hung up the phone, she reread some of the dialogue for the next day's rehearsal. She thought that maybe if everybody saw how good she was, that would change their minds, and they'd stop harassing her with those notes.

She would prove that a Vietnamese girl could be the best Lady Macbeth anybody had ever seen.

Kim thought about Tyler then. He was being so nice and attentive. Kim feared he might be falling in love with her or something. She would hate for that to happen because he would end up getting hurt. She decided she would have to gently make it clear to him that Huong was firmly in her heart.

....

On Wednesday when there was no play rehearsal, Kim went to work at the day care center. She worked with the children on more complicated origami figures. This time they made goldfish, which required many more folds. The goldfish turned out very beautiful, and the children squealed with delight.

Kim worried about the walk home in the dark, but she refused to allow herself to become a prisoner of fear. Anyway, there was no reason to believe anyone would actually harm her. The other cast members of *Macbeth* just wanted to get her out of the play. They weren't trying to kill her!

As Kim walked, she became aware of a pickup truck on the street beside her. It rattled in a very familiar way. It was Huong's old pickup truck, the one he used in his part time jobs, hauling trash and doing garden work for neighbors to raise college money.

"Hi, Kim," he shouted. "Hop in."

Kim climbed into the cab of the truck.

"You want to stop for a strawberry shake?" Huong asked. He seemed to want to talk to Kim so she agreed.

They pulled into the hamburger place and ordered two strawberry shakes. As they sat in the truck sipping them, Kim said, "What a coincidence that you were just driving by, Huong."

"No," Huong admitted. "I was parked across from your day care center waiting for you. I wanted to talk to you."

"We were both in school all day," Kim said.

Huong was not wearing his usual happy smile. "Kim, today very late in the day, somebody told me something that shook me up big time. Somebody said you told them you feel trapped in our relationship. And that you'd like to see other people."

Kim almost dropped her strawberry shake. "Huong, who told you that?" she demanded.

"I don't want to say, Kim, but I just want to make sure it's not true. I wouldn't ever want you to feel trapped in our friendship or obligated to me if you stopped enjoying being with me," Huong said.

"Huong, whoever told you that is a liar and a troublemaker," Kim said. "Huong, I sometimes think I am falling to pieces. Everywhere I turn people are lying about me and trying to undermine me! I feel sometimes like I'm losing my mind. I think sometimes someone is trying to make me crazy." Warm tears streamed down Kim's face.

Huong reached out and put his arms around Kim, and she sobbed into his chest. Between sobs, Kim poured out all the misfortunes that had been happening to her in the past few weeks.

Hatred flowed quickly into Huong's eyes, too quickly. Kim remembered what Tyler had said about Huong being a hothead. "That is so evil, Kim," Huong said. "Who is behind all this?"

"I don't know," Kim cried.

9 WHEN KIM AND ARNETTA were shopping at the mall on Saturday, they spotted Rodney and Pamela walking along, hand in hand. "Look," Arnetta said bitterly, "the two phonies are going in that expensive ice cream store."

"He really wanted Pamela to be Lady Macbeth," Kim said.

"Tough. Mr. Gabriel picked the best actress, and he had better deal with it," Arnetta snapped.

As Kim and Arnetta were passing the ice cream store, Rodney and Pamela were coming out. They all arrived awkwardly at the same spot. Kim hadn't wanted to meet them, but she couldn't avoid it. They were right in front of her.

"Hi, Kim," Pamela sang out in her breezy voice. "Man, the prices in there are outrageous! One stupid little ice cream cone costs a fortune."

"A real rip-off," Rodney said.

Kim looked at the two smiling and being cordial to her while in their hearts they hated her. It was almost too much to bear. But Kim struggled to be polite. "We always buy our ice cream cones at the hamburger place. They're really cheap, and you get a lot of nice, soft ice cream," Kim said.

"Hey, that's a great idea," Rodney said. "Let's go over there and get cones. Kim, Arnetta, join us."

Arnetta looked at Kim. Kim shrugged and said, "Okay."

The three girls and Rodney ordered ice cream cones and sat in a booth eating them.

"I'm getting to love playing a witch," Pamela giggled. "I never knew it could be so much fun."

Kim tried to concentrate on her ice cream cone. She kept asking herself, over and over, how could they act so normal when they were plotting against her?

"I'll tell you something about this girl here," Rodney said, looking at Kim. "When she was chosen to play Lady Macbeth, I was pretty ticked off. I thought, is this sweet little thing going to be able to do mean old Lady Macbeth? But, Kim, you've amazed me. Mr. Gabriel told me the other day that you've turned out even better than he had hoped."

Kim stared at the handsome young man. Tyler's words came back to her. She had asked if Rodney was part of the conspiracy against her. Oh yeah, Tyler had said quickly. Especially him.

Now, here was Rodney smiling and lavishing praise on Kim.

"Girl," Arnetta said, "there's a reason we're all right here, right now. It's time for some straight talk."

"Arnetta is right," Kim said. "I've been getting these hateful notes and phone calls telling me to drop out of the play. The notes aren't signed. Some coward starts out by quoting Shakespeare, then the rest of it is a threat against me."

"Kim was told that some of you guys from the cast are responsible for the threats," Arnetta chimed in. "Because you don't want her playing Lady Macbeth."

Rodney looked shocked. Or perhaps, as a very good actor, he was feigning shock. "Kim, this is unbelievable!" he cried. "Have you talked to Mr. Gabriel about it?"

"I did at first, but he thought it was just

some clown playing a joke. But the notes kept coming and other stuff too. A flower box filled with garbage and a paper skeleton hanging from the day care window where I work," Kim said. "Then somebody told me that the cast of *Macbeth* is trying to get me to drop out of the play."

"That's a filthy, rotten lie," Rodney said in his best Macbeth voice. Other people eating nearby looked up, startled. "I've never heard anything so stupid in my life! If I had any problem with you playing Lady Macbeth, I would have talked to you about it. If I was sure you were going to harm the play, then I would have withdrawn myself so as not to be associated with a dud!"

"Yeah," Pamela said, "what kind of a creep told you something like that, Kim? Everybody in the cast likes you! It must be somebody trying to wreck the play by turning us all against each other."

"I can't tell you who told me," Kim said. "It would just cause more trouble."

"Oh, splendid," Rodney said, rolling his eyes. "Heaven forbid we unmask the fool!"

Kim didn't know what to believe. As she walked from the mall with Arnetta, she asked, "What do you think?"

"I'm not sure, Kim, but you need to go back to Tyler and find out exactly what he heard," Arnetta said.

....

When Kim walked up the flagstone walk leading to the Kern house on Monday afternoon, she noticed all the blinds were closed. She hadn't seen Tyler in school all day, and now she wondered if he was sick or something.

Mrs. Kern came to answer the door. "Oh dear," she said, seeming distressed, "I didn't know Tyler asked you over this afternoon. I would have baked some cookies if I'd known. I have a dentist's appointment in a while, so there's no time to do it now."

"Please, Mrs. Kern, there's no need. I didn't tell Tyler I was coming over. I didn't see him in school . . . is he all right?" Kim said.

"Tyler wasn't feeling well this morning, but now he's out doing some grocery shopping. He should be back soon. Why don't you come in and wait for him, dear?" Mrs. Kern led the way into the living room and fluffed out a pillow on a chair, motioning for Kim to sit down.

As Kim sat down, she noticed a portrait on the opposite wall. It was of a fine-looking man, about 40, who bore a close resemblance to Tyler.

"Is that Tyler's dad?" Kim asked.

Mrs. Kern flinched. "Did Tyler tell you about his father?" she asked in a careful voice.

"Yes, he did," Kim said. "It was very sad."

"Did Tyler tell you everything?" Mrs. Kern asked.

"Yes," Kim said.

"Then there's no need for my little white lie. I don't actually have a dental appointment. I'm going to visit my husband now. I visit him as much as I can, but it's a very long trip, and visiting hours are limited. There's so much hassle . . . "

Kim was puzzled. If Mr. Kern was in a hospital, visiting hours should be liberal. Last year one of Kim's friends was in the hospital and Kim visited any time during the day, several times a week. "It's nice that you visit him," Kim said. "Tyler seems to care very much for his father."

"He was Tyler's hero. They did just about everything together. They camped in the mountains and went deep-sea fishing. They even went to Japan one year, just the two of them, and they had a ball. My husband . . . was a wonderful father. Short-tempered at times, but so very good with Tyler." The woman trembled visibly. "It was such a horrendous tragedy. Nobody saw it coming . . . least of all me."

"Is there any chance he'll be better soon and can come home?" Kim asked.

Mrs. Kern looked shocked. "You said Tyler told you everything!" she said.

"Well, yes, he told me how his father was harassed at work and how your family suffered. He told me that," Kim said.

Mrs. Kern seemed to shrivel up before Kim's eyes. "Yes," she said. "We suffered very much. But it happened over two years ago. We are getting better. There will eventually be—what's that word? Closure. Yes, closure. Well, Tyler will be back soon. There are cookies in the cupboard. Store-bought. Not the good ones, but they'll have to do." She looked at her watch. "I'd better be going. Bye now."

Tyler came home about 15 minutes later. "Kim!" he said in surprise when he saw her.

"Your mom let me in," Kim said. "She said I could wait for you. I need to talk to you, Tyler."

"Sure. You look really stressed, Kim. You look like you've been through the wringer. You look like you've reached the breaking point, Kim," Tyler said.

10

"I'M ALL RIGHT, TYLER," Kim said.

"Your eyes. They've got big, dark circles under them," Tyler said. "And you look like you've lost weight too. Man, those creeps in the cast are getting their way. They're running you right into the ground."

Kim did not believe she looked that bad. Surely her parents would have noticed and said something. Kim thought she was handling all this pretty well. "I'm really okay, Tyler. I can take a lot. I've told you, I come from a really strong family. I told you how my father survived the terrible trip from the China Sea. His life was not easy when he came here either. But he never let anything stop him. That's in my blood too," Kim said.

"Nobody can take stress that doesn't quit," Tyler said. "Nobody." He seemed almost angry that Kim was insisting she was all right. "I don't care how brave you are. When they just keep coming at you,

you break. Everybody has a breaking point. My father was a strong man too. You should have seen him sport fishing and dragging in those big tuna. He did a lot of great things. He was a terrific guy. I thought he was Superman. But they broke him. If they could break him, then anybody can be broken."

"I'm sure your father is a fine man. Your mother told me that she's going to visit him today. Do you go often too, Tyler?" Kim asked.

Tyler paled. His mouth worked but no words came for a few minutes. Then he said, "My mother told you where he was?"

"No. She just said visiting hours were limited, and I felt bad about that. Most hospitals let you in most of the time during the day," Kim said.

"I'm glad you stopped by, Kim," Tyler said, abruptly changing the subject. "You won't believe what I heard those rotten creeps in the *Macbeth* cast talking about. They want to push you over the edge quickly now, so Pamela can start rehearsing with the cast as Lady Macbeth. They're going to send you down to the basement to get some props, and then they're going to rig the door and slam it on you. There you'll be, trapped in that musty old closet with no lights.

"But that's not the worst of it. They're going to get some rats from the biology lab and stick them in there with you . . . " A fine sheen of perspiration glowed on Tyler's face. His eyes looked strange.

Kim began to be afraid. She was planning on telling him that she had talked to Rodney and Pamela about all this. But now Kim decided not to do that.

There was something wrong with Tyler, something terribly wrong.

"I just wanted to ask you how you are coming with Macduff, Tyler," Kim said.

"What?" Tyler asked, disbelief on his face. "You're wondering how I'm doing with Macduff when your whole world is collapsing around your head? Your boyfriend hates you. I talked to him, and he said he just wants his freedom. He said he was tired of you guys always being together. I didn't want to tell you all of it, with everything else going wrong, but the truth is, nobody likes you, Kim. Beth hates you and so do Rodney and Pamela. They're all out to get you . . . "

"I'm sorry about that," Kim said. She was growing more nervous by the minute. "I need to go home now and think about all this."

"I'll drive you home," Tyler said.

"No, no, today is such a nice day," Kim said. "I'll enjoy the walk." She headed for the door.

Tyler hurried alongside her. "Kim, I'm worried about you. You just look so much like my father did before he cracked. I'm afraid you're going across the street to the school auditorium to just trash everything. I wouldn't blame you. Nobody would. They've just pushed you too far. Anybody can see that . . . "

Kim noticed that the young man was trembling violently now. "It's all right, Tyler," Kim said, staring longingly at the door. Tyler was blocking her way now. "I'll be all right, Tyler. I just need to go home."

"Don't go," Tyler pleaded. "Please don't go, Kim. Just stay a little while."

"All right," Kim said. She sat on the edge of a chair, and he sat on the sofa opposite her. He clasped his hands to keep them from shaking.

"He's in prison," Tyler said.

Kim didn't say anything. She assumed Tyler meant his father, but she didn't say a word.

"They made it look like he was a monster," Tyler said. "A bloody monster. My dad. He was such a great guy. During the trial, it was in all the papers. Guys would point to me at school. Our friends turned away from us. But he wasn't a monster. He was my dad . . . and I loved him. He was the best dad a kid ever had . . . "

"I believe you," Kim said softly.

Tyler stared at her. "I didn't want to hurt you. I swear I didn't. I'm really sorry about everything. But, I had to prove to myself that my dad wasn't a monster, that if you hassle a good person long enough they'll break. I wanted to prove to myself that even a really nice person like you would snap and go a little crazy," he said.

Kim looked at the boy in silence. Horror gripped her, but she kept it from her face.

"I wrote all those notes. I turned Beth against you. I hung the paper skeleton on

the window of that place where you work.
I even sent the garbage in the flower box. I
thought you'd freak and then, see, it would
mean that my dad wasn't a monster just
because he couldn't take it anymore.

"At my dad's trial, the prosecutor said
really good things about the other guys,
like they were angels. But when he talked
about my dad . . . he said . . . he said,
'there is pure evil.' You understand, Kim?
They were talking about my dad, and they
wouldn't cut him any slack even though
they were the ones hassling him." Tyler
began speaking between dry sobs.

"I'm very sorry, Tyler," Kim said.

"The court dug up all the bad stuff they
could on my dad, so they could convince
the jury how evil he was. Some little fight
he had been in years before, everything.
But those other guys . . . the guys he shot,
the prosecutor had nothing but good things
to say about them . . . " Tyler said.

Kim stiffened.

"The guys he shot?"

Kim felt as if someone had spilled ice
down her back.

"They said my dad was the worst. Our

lawyer, he got a doctor who explained about how people sometimes snap when the pressure gets to be too much, but nobody wanted to hear that. Nobody. So they convicted him. Murder One—life without parole. No hope, Kim. Nada." Tyler lowered his head and buried his face in his hands.

Kim wanted to bolt for the door and just get out of there. But she said, "Tyler, maybe it would help if you talked to somebody, like a counselor. You said you maybe wanted to be a psychologist someday. Well, maybe one of them can help you now . . . "

Tyler looked up. "Everybody has a breaking point. I thought you'd rip up the costumes, ruin the play. But you didn't. You took it all, and you . . . didn't break. So maybe my dad is a monster."

"Everybody is different," Kim said. "Everybody has a different breaking point."

"He shot three guys," Tyler said. "One of them died. He went through the office like a madman, kicking in doors. That's why they called him a monster . . . "

"Nobody is a monster," Kim said.

"Nobody who is so loved by his son could be a monster."

"How do you know I still love him?" Tyler asked.

"You do, don't you?" Kim said.

Tyler nodded.

Kim briefly laid her hand on his shoulder, then she turned and left the house.

The darkness of night was descending slowly, but to Kim it seemed like midday. The sun was shining. Her heart felt lighter. She felt very sorry for Tyler, but she was so grateful to discover that the cast of *Macbeth* was on her side, and her friends still loved her. Life was good again.